My First
Kitten

by Karla Olson

Illustrated by Diane Blasius

Andrews and McMeel
A Universal Press Syndicate Company
Kansas City

ISBN 0-8362-4232-7

MY FIRST KITTEN was prepared and produced by Magnolia Editions
Limited, 15 West 26th Street, New York, New York 10010

Editors: Sharyn Rosart, Loretta Mowat
Art Director: Jeff Batzli
Designer: Jennifer S. Markson

Published in the United States by Andrews and McMeel Publishing Co.,
4900 Main Street, Kansas City, Missouri 64112

Attention: Schools and Businesses
Andrews and McMeel books are available at quantity discounts with bulk
purchase for educational, business, or sales promotional use.
For information, please write to:
Special Sales Department, Andrews and McMeel,
4900 Main Street, Kansas City, Missouri 64112.

Contents Kaitlyn

Introduction

YOU'VE FINALLY GOT A FLUFFY, FRISKY, ADORABLE KITTEN to cuddle, love, and keep healthy and happy all of its life!

My First Kitten tells how to care for your kitten, from making sure your home is safe to feeding, grooming, and playing. Also included is a fun diary section to record things you want to remember about your kitten.

After you choose your kitten's name, write it and your phone number on the I.D. tag that comes with this book, insert it into the purple heart with the name facing the flat side, and hang it on your kitten's collar.  That way, your kitten will be returned to you if it ever gets lost. The special heart will also reflect streetlights and headlights at night and help keep your kitten safe.

Start today to love and care for your kitten, and in return, your kitten will purr for you, play with you, and love you every day for the rest of its life.

Welcome Home Kitty!

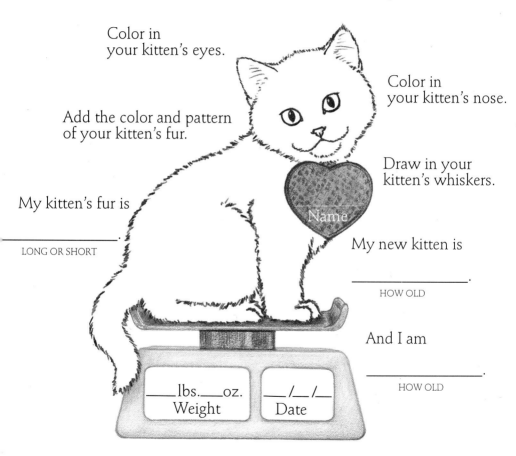

Color in
your kitten's eyes.

Color in
your kitten's nose.

Add the color and pattern
of your kitten's fur.

Draw in your
kitten's whiskers.

Name

My kitten's fur is

_____.

LONG OR SHORT

My new kitten is

_____.

HOW OLD

And I am

_____.

HOW OLD

____lbs.____oz.
Weight

__/__/__
Date

Your Kitten's Home

Make sure your home is safe and comfortable for your kitten. Sit down with your parents and answer the following questions.

🐾 Where will you keep your kitten's litter pan?

🐾 Where will your kitten sleep?

🐾 Is your house safe for a kitten? See "Kittenproofing" for help to make sure.

🐾 Where will you keep your kitten when you are not home so it won't get into trouble?

KITTENPROOFING

Here's how to kittenproof your home:

- Close off any areas where your kitten shouldn't go, including behind the stove and refrigerator.
- Remove anything breakable.
- Add screens to all windows.
- Remove poisonous plants. Ask your vet for a list.
- Close all cupboards and drawers.
- Always close the washing machine and dryer.

INSIDE, OUTSIDE

There are many things lurking outside–cars, other animals, and other cats, who may carry infectious diseases such as feline leukemia—that make the outdoors dangerous. If you keep your kitten inside from the very start, it won't miss being outside at all. Just make sure you spend a little time–at least 15 to 30 minutes every day–playing with your kitten so it gets some exercise.

What Kind of Cat Is That?

There are many different kinds of cats, though they look more alike than different kinds of dogs. Here are some:

Domestics Domestics are the most common kind of cat. They have long or short hair in many colors and patterns:

One color all over

Two colors

Tabby –stripes, swirls, or patches.

Tortoiseshell –orange, black, and tan all mixed up.

Calico –orange, black, tan, and white.

Tipped or pointed –light body with dark face, ears, paws, and tail.

Purebreds Here are some of the most popular purebreds:

> **Persian** –long fluffy hair and a flat face. Not a playful cat, but quiet and calm. Requires daily grooming.

> **Siamese** –light-colored, thin body with points. Smart, talkative, and loyal.

> **Maine Coon** –big, sturdy cat with a fluffy coat that needs grooming. Very active and curious.

CAT FACT
If you chose a particular kind of kitten–a Persian or a Siamese, for instance–you chose a pure-bred, a kitten whose grandparents and parents looked just like it. Most kittens are cross-bred, which means that their grandparents and parents were all different colors, patterns, and kinds.

Kitty Paraphernalia

Here's what you need to care for your kitten.

Litter pan, litter, pan liners, and litter scoop

Food bowl and water dish

Food

Scratching post or pad

Cat carrier

Cat brush

Metal comb

Cotton balls

Collar (with an elastic insert, so kitty won't choke if its collar catches on a branch, and a place to hang your kitten's reflective ID tag)

Toys
Store Bought

Suede or felt mouse

Ball with a bell inside

Kitty Tease –looks like a fishing rod with a bow on the end

Homemade

Foil ball

Paper ball

Film canister with a bell inside

Paper bag

Empty box

Ball of yarn

Your shadow

KITTEN CARE FOR EVERY DAY

Here are six things your kitten would ask you to do every day:

🐾 Feed me

🐾 Change my water

🐾 Groom me

🐾 Play with me

🐾 Clean out my litter pan

🐾 Cuddle me

11

What to Expect the First Night

Remember that this is probably your kitten's first night away from its family and that it hasn't been to many new places. Be very gentle.

🐾 Keep your kitten in one room for the first few days.

🐾 Show your kitten the litter pan right away.

🐾 Set down a bowl of water.

🐾 Keep other pets away for a few days, then introduce them one at a time. Stay in the room while they meet.

🐾 Wait a week or so to take your kitten to show and tell or to meet your friends.

🐾 Your kitten will be up early ready to ramble and make mischief. Now is a fun time to get to know it.

CAT FACT
Cats sleep about sixteen hours a day, but they have good reason for being so lazy. In the wild, they sometimes go several days between meals. They sleep to save energy for the next hunt.

HOW TO HOLD A KITTEN

Hold your kitten with both hands, one in front with your fingers on either side of its legs, and the other around its rear end. Never hold onto a kitten when it wants to get away–let it go. If you don't, it won't want to come back to you. Never pick your kitten up by the skin around its neck.

KITTY COMFORT

Your kitten will probably wake up and meow during the night, looking for its family. Pick up your kitten and let it know that you will be its family now. If your kitten is still upset, put a ticking clock or a hot water bottle wrapped in a towel in its bed. The tick of the clock will remind your kitten of its mother's heartbeat and the hot water bottle the warm body of its brother or sister.

13

Games to Play with Your Kitten

Bottle Cap Hockey: Send your kitten scooting around the room after a bottle cap.

Flashlight Tag: Wave the beam of a flashlight at a wall and watch your kitten chase it.

CAT FACT
Does your kitten crouch, stalk, and spring at you? In the wild, cats are hunters, capturing the food they eat. Your kitten is practicing!

Kitty Pong: Roll a ping pong ball across the floor. Your kitten will knock it around.

Bedsheet Tent Town: Spread an old sheet over the bed with the kitten underneath. Run your hand over the sheet. Your kitten will chase your hand and put its feet in the air, making a tent.

Bag Tag: Lay several paper grocery bags on the floor. Your kitten will dive into one. Tap the bag and it will race out and dive into another.

Air Kitten: Stand up and dangle a ribbon about waist-high. Your kitten will leap for it; you'll be amazed at how high!

CAT FACT

A cat has 244 bones (38 more than you do), and they are connected by muscles instead of ligaments like ours. This means a cat can almost move each bone individually, which is why it can curl up so tight, stretch so long, jump so high, and move so quickly.

15

Feeding Your Kitten

By the time you get your kitten it should be eating cat food, not just mother's milk.

Your kitten will eat 4 to 6 small meals a day. Offer it about a tablespoon at a time. Let your kitten eat what it wants, then throw away whatever is left.

Things You Should Never Feed Your Kitten

Dog food

Chocolate –Kittens are allergic to it, poor things.

Milk –It may give your kitten diarrhea. Yuck!

Small brittle bones –Your kitten can choke on them.

Leftovers

WHAT'S COOKIN'?
Cat food comes three ways–wet (canned), semi-moist (in an envelope), and dry (in a box or bag). Ask your vet which kind he or she recommends.

16

Treat for Your Cat

About half of all cats adore catnip. They roll in it and eat it, then scamper and play. A little while later they sleep so deeply you'll have a hard time waking them.

CAT FACT

Cats are carnivores, which means they eat mostly meat, but they also like vegetables and plants, such as grass.

TEN THINGS YOU SHOULD NEVER DO TO YOUR CAT

Never hit your cat.

Never kick your cat.

Never drop your cat from your arms; set it down gently.

Never pull your cat's tail.

Never pick your cat up by the skin around its neck.

Never keep holding your cat when it wants to get down.

Never tease your cat or it won't trust you.

Never leave your cat out at night.

Never wake your cat suddenly; speak to it first.

Never feed your cat from your plate.

17

Name That Kitten

Think about names before you go to pick out your kitten, but don't make the final decision until you meet it. Choose a name that is easy to say (so you can call your kitten) and not like every other kitten's (so only your kitten comes when you call).

🐾 Choose a name that fits your kitten because of its color or a special feature:

Midnight (black), **Blizzard** (white), **Smudge** (grey), **Shades** (dark circles around the eyes).

🐾 Choose a name that describes your kitten's personality:

Giggles (makes you laugh), **Beans** (jumps like a Mexican jumpingbean), **Sweetpea** (curls up in your lap).

Name your kitten after your favorite character from a movie or book:

Sylvester (loves chasing birds), **Aladdin** (flies through the air), **Cruella** (is up to no good), **Tom** (hangs out with a mouse).

Choose a word you like that fits your kitten:

Xerox (a copycat), **Chopstick** (long, thin, and quick), **Gadget** (a bundle of energy), **Rebound** (always bounces back).

Litter-training Your Kitten

Your kitten's mother should have taught it how to use the litter pan. If your kitten is not quite sure what to do, here's how to show it.

🐾 While your kitten is awake, set it in the litter pan once every hour. It will probably scramble out, but when it uses the pan, praise and cuddle the kitten.

🐾 In between, watch for signs that your kitten has to go–digging in a corner or at the newspaper. Set the kitten in the pan, then praise it when it is done.

Scoop out dirty litter at least once a day.

Clean up any mistakes made outside the pan very carefully. If your kitten smells the spot later, it may go there again.

Don't scold your kitten unless you catch it in the act. It won't understand and will become afraid of you.

Grooming Your Kitten

Your kitten's mother taught it to keep clean, but it'll appreciate some help.

🐾 Groom your kitten as soon as you get it so it gets used to grooming.

🐾 If your kitten is long-haired, groom it every day; a short-haired kitten, about three times a week.

🐾 First, gently brush your kitten all over with the pet brush. Stroke in the same direction as the fur.

🐾 Next, comb very gently through the coat with the metal comb. Untangle any knots with your fingers.

CAT FACT

Have you noticed that your kitten always cleans itself after it eats? And does your kitten sometimes do it near you? Grooming is a social activity, which is why your kitten likes it so much when you help.

🐾 Finally, use a cotton ball to clean away any dirt on the inside of your kitten's ears, but not down in the ear; this area cleans itself.

🐾 Have an adult look at your kitten's claws and clip them if they are long. Stand by to pet and cuddle your kitten.

🐾 In the spring, your kitten will shed its winter coat. Be especially careful to help your kitten groom then.

WELL-KITTEN CHECKLIST FOR ONCE A WEEK

Look your kitten over from head to tail. If you see anything funny, show an adult. Check:

Eyes   Ears
Nose   Coat
Claws and pads

🐾 Remember to change the litter and wash out the litter pan once a week, too.

Kitten Speak

A cat talks with its voice, but also its eyes, ears, tail, fur, and whole body. Here's what your kitten may be saying:

Voice
Happy: meows, trills, chirps, and purrs
Unhappy: yowls, hisses, growls, and snarls

Eyes
Happy: sleepy, half closed
Alert: wide open, small pupils
Scared or angry: wide open, big pupils

Ears
Alert: pricked up
Angry: pulled down flat

CAT FACT
House cats are the only animals that can purr, a sound like a little rumble in the tummy. Lions and their wild relatives can't do it! How cats purr is still a mystery, though everyone knows why they do it–because they are happy, comfortable, and loved!

Whole Body

Happy: relaxed and comfortable with smooth fur
Angry: arched up with puffed fur
Scared: crouched

Tail

Happy: held high
Excited: twitching
Scared: bushy

WAYS YOUR KITTEN SAYS "I LOVE YOU"

🐾 Greets you with a trill or chirp and an upraised tail.

🐾 Rubs up against your leg.

🐾 Rubs you with its head.

🐾 Curls its tail around your leg.

🐾 Licks your hand, arm, or leg.

WAYS YOU CAN TALK TO YOUR KITTEN

🐾 Use its name.

🐾 Cuddle it and say "good kitty" when it does something you like.

🐾 Say "no" in a growly voice when it does something bad.

🐾 Never hit your kitten.

Kitten Astrology

Even if you don't know exactly when your kitten was born, you probably have an idea of how old it is. Count back to its birthday.

Aries
March 21-April 19
Energetic and friendly; loves to be the center of attention.

Cancer
June 22-July 22
Gentle and a little shy; likes to stick around home.

Taurus
April 20-May 20
Gentle, but strong; a great playmate.

Leo
July 23-August 22
Active, curious; a very good watchcat.

Gemini
May 21-June 21
Curious and excited– sometimes a little too excited!

Virgo
August 23-September 22
Will amuse you with tricks and games.

Libra
September 23-October 23
Will fit right into your family; everybody's best friend.

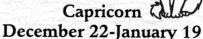

Capricorn
December 22-January 19
Easygoing and a little shy; loves high places, such as your shoulder.

Scorpio
October 24-November 21
Very possessive of toys and territory; intensely loyal.

Aquarius
January 20-February 18
Will get into everything; very talkative.

Sagittarius
November 22-December 21
Fun-loving and friendly; always a kitten at heart.

Pisces
February 19-March 20
Calm, gentle, and very quiet; likes to stick around home.

Fascinating Feline Facts

The average male cat weighs 8 pounds 6 ounces, and the average female 7 pounds 2 ounces. Most males live to be 13 to 15 years old, and most females 15 to 17. Remember this while you read these amazing facts and stories, but don't try them on your own kitten.

The smallest cat ever weighed 1 pound 8 ounces and was 10 inches long.

The largest cat weighed 46 pounds 15¼ ounces and was 38 inches long, with a 15-inch neck and a 33-inch waist.

The oldest cat known is Puss, who lived to be 36.

In 1986, Victa spent 12 hours in the refrigerator. Everyone thought she was dead until–suddenly–she got up and walked away!

Sugar was left in California when her owners moved to Oklahoma. Fourteen months later, Sugar turned up on her owners' doorstep. She had traveled 1500 miles to a place she'd never been!

Cat Poems

Three Tabbies
KATE GREENAWAY

Three tabbies took out their cats to tea,
As well-behaved tabbies as well could be:
Each sat in the chair that each preferred,
They mewed for their milk, and they sipped and purred.
Now tell me this (as these cats you've seen them)–
How many lives had these cats between them?

Two Poems
OLIVER HERFORD

When Human Folk at Table eat,
A Kitten must not mew for meat,
Or Jump to grab it from the Dish,
(Unless it happens to be fish).

To Someone very Good and Just,
Who has proved worthy of her trust,
A Cat will sometimes condescend–
The Dog is Everybody's friend.

30

Jokes Your Kitten Will Love

What's the opposite of a cool cat?
A hot dog.

What do you call a kitten that loves lemons?
A sour puss.

What is a kitten's favorite play?
Ro-meow and Juliet.

What is every kitten's favorite TV show?
The A-cat-emy Awards.

Why can't a kitten watch movies on the VCR?
Because all it can use is paws.

Why do kittens always go to their fathers?
They always land on their paws.

A Trip to the Vet

Take your new kitten to the vet as soon as you can. Even if it got shots before you picked it up (be sure to ask), you will want your vet to check your kitten over. Use the "Patient Chart" below to keep track of what the vet says.

Patient Chart

Patient's name:_____ Sex:_____ Age:_____

Food prescribed:_____

How much?_____ How often?_____

Medicines prescribed:_____ Dose:_____

Tests taken:_____ Results:_____

When should patient be altered?_____

Training tips for patient:_____

Rabies Vaccination Certificate given:_____

NOTE: Your town may require a Rabies Vaccination Certificate to prove that your kitten had a rabies shot. Be sure you get this from your vet.

Immunization Chart

Vet's Name:_____
Address:_____
Phone:_____

Whenever the vet gives your kitten a shot, ask what it is for and when your kitten needs to have another one, then write it down on this chart.

Date	Shot	Next Shot Needed

ALTERING YOUR CAT

When he or she is about six months old, have your kitten altered–called spaying for a female and neutering for a male. This prevents your cat from having a litter of kittens, and will make your cat a better friend and you a responsible pet owner. There are already too many kittens in the world without homes. Don't let your cat make more.

My Kitten Diary

My kitten is six months old.

Now my kitten is as big as_____.

My kitten weighs_____pounds_____ounces.
                       HOW MANY   HOW MANY

My kitten's favorite place to sleep is_____.

My kitten talks to me when_____.

My kitten purrs when_____.

My kitten's favorite toy is_____.

My kitten's favorite game is_____.

The funniest thing my kitten did lately is_____.

My kitten is one year old.
My kitten is a cat!

Now my cat is as big as_____.

My cat weighs _____pounds_____ounces.
                 HOW MANY   HOW MANY

My cat's favorite place to sleep is_____.

My cat talks to me when_____.

My cat purrs when_____.

My cat's favorite toy is_____.

My cat's favorite game is_____.

The funniest thing my cat did lately is_____.